Thornberrys

All Washed Up

by Michele Spirn
illustrated by Steve Haefele

Simon Spotlight/Nickelodeon
New York   London   Toronto   Sydney   Singapore

Discovery Facts

Arabian Peninsula (uh RAY bee an pen IN sue la): The Arabian Peninsula is made up of seven countries: Saudi Arabia, Kuwait, Bahrain, Qatar, the United Arab Emirates, Oman, and Yemen. It is surrounded by water on three sides. There are huge deserts at the northern end. During the summer (May through September) it can be very hot—up to 120 degrees Fahrenheit during the day. Sometimes there are heavy rains which can flood valleys quickly.

Caracal (KAR a kal): A medium-sized cat that lives in Africa, Asia, and the Arabian Peninsula. It is very fast and can leap high in the air to catch birds. The caracal also eats small mammals. A caracal looks different from household cats because it has very long ears with long black hair sticking up from the tips. Its name comes from a Turkish word meaning "black ear."

Myrrh (MURR): A large bush that grows as tall as nine feet. It has been around for thousands of years. The sap that comes from the plant can be used to make soap and perfume. When burned, the smell chases mosquitoes away.

KLASKY CSUPO INC.

Based on the TV series *The Wild Thornberrys*® created by Klasky Csupo, Inc. as seen on Nickelodeon®

SIMON SPOTLIGHT
An imprint of Simon & Schuster Children's Publishing Division
1230 Avenue of the Americas, New York, New York 10020

"Let's go, Marianne," called Nigel. "We've got to get out early if we want to catch that cheetah on film."

"Coming, Nigel," said Marianne.

"But, Mom," said Debbie, "it's *my* birthday! You haven't forgotten, have you?"

"Of course not," said Marianne. "We'll be back by three o'clock. Right, Nigel?"

"Abso-totally-lutely," said Nigel. "Three it is. Ta ta."

"What a life!" Debbie exclaimed. "I've run out of shampoo. My perfume dried up. I'm in a cosmetics wasteland! Whoa! Where are you two going?"

"We'll be back soon," said Eliza. "C'mon, Darwin!"

"Now *you're* leaving me alone too! And on my birthday!"

"Donnie's here," said Eliza.

"Oh yeah. I'll have lots of chuckles with nature boy!"

"What's the rush?" asked Darwin, as he ran after Eliza.

"I ordered Debbie some new perfume for her birthday," said Eliza. "But it didn't come yet. Now I have to find something else!"

"Where?" asked Darwin. "It's not as if there's a shopping mall handy. Besides, it's starting to rain."

"What about bushes of myrrh?" asked Eliza, frantically thumbing through her book, *Plants of the Desert*.

"Are they good to eat like Cheese Munchies?" asked Darwin.

"No, but you can make perfume and soap out of myrrh," replied Eliza. "It's supposed to be right here in the Arabian Peninsula."

"What does myrrh look like?" asked Darwin.
"It can be as tall as nine feet high," said Eliza.
"How will you get the leaves?" asked Darwin.
Eliza looked at him.
"Uh-oh, not me," said Darwin. "Really, Eliza, a climb like that is way too dangerous!"

"All right. I'll get the myrrh. But you have to help me find it," said Eliza.

"Fine, but now it's raining hard," Darwin replied. "Wait, what's that sound?"

Eliza looked behind her and saw a wall of water coming toward them. "Run, Darwin!" she shrieked. She grabbed him and raced into a cave nearby.

"Whew! That was close!" exclaimed Darwin. "What was that?"

"A flash flood!" Eliza answered.

"But we're in the desert! There's *not* supposed to be much water," said Darwin.

"Incorrect, little furry mammal," barked a sharp voice. "Rains cause floods here."

"Aaargh!" screamed Darwin as he jumped into Eliza's arms. She backed toward the opening of the cave and looked out. The whole valley was flooded with water!

"We're sorry to bother you," said Eliza politely.

"No bother, big animal," barked the voice. "Plenty of room."

"I am Eliza and this is my friend Darwin. Who are you? You sound like a dog."

"Not a dog," replied the voice.

"If you're not a dog, what are you?" asked Eliza. "Come out, please, where we can see you."

"Promise not to hurt me?" the voice asked.

"Of course," said Eliza.

"Here I am," announced the voice.

"You look like a cat," said Eliza.

"Yes. I am a caracal," said the animal. "A hungry caracal."

"What do caracals eat?" asked Eliza.

"Birds. Little furry mammals," answered the caracal, licking her mouth.

"You're not going to eat me," said Darwin, clinging to Eliza.

"Hmm, you'd be a big mouthful," said the caracal.

"Let's get out of here," Darwin pleaded, pulling on Eliza.

"We're trapped. The water hasn't gone down enough," whispered Eliza, looking outside.

Eliza turned to the caracal and said, "I've got an idea. Darwin has something for you to eat."

She looked at Darwin's Cheese Munchies.

"Not my precious Cheese Munchies," he wailed.

"Darwin, will you please share your Munchies?" asked Eliza.

"Eliza, we could be trapped here for hours," Darwin whispered. "If we give away these Cheese Munchies, we'll have nothing to eat. We'll waste away!"

"The Commvee is just up the hill, Darwin," answered Eliza. "We'll be back soon. Besides, she's hungry, and we have food."

"Here," said Eliza, tearing a Cheese Munchie away from Darwin. "Hope you like it."

The caracal tasted it. "Mmm. Not bad. I want some more."

"Have all you want," gulped Darwin. He peered out of the cave nervously. "Hooray! Water's down. Time to leave. Thanks for your hospitality." He grabbed Eliza's hand.

Eliza looked at her watch. "Oh, no! It's almost three o'clock! I still have to find a birthday present for my sister," she explained to the caracal. "Have you seen any myrrh?"

"There was some. None now," said the caracal as she glanced outside the cave.

"The flood's washed everything away!" cried Eliza. "What'll I do?"

"Good luck," said the caracal.

"We could give Debbie some Cheese Munchies and say they're from both of us," suggested Darwin.

"That's really nice of you," said Eliza, "but I have to give her something from me."

"Eliza, where have you been?" asked Marianne. "We're ready to surprise Debbie. I made a necklace and a banana cake for her."

"And I've smoked her some fish," said Nigel. "They taste delightfully like kippers."

"I ordered something but it never came," said Eliza.

"I'm sure Debbie will understand," said Nigel.

"Yeah, right," said Eliza.

"Donnie, come down!" called Marianne.

"I'll get him, Mom," said Eliza. As she and Darwin walked over to the bush, she clutched Darwin's arm.

"Darwin, do you know what *that* is?" she asked.

"Well, it's a tree, or a bush. Green, leaves, tall . . . about nine feet. Is that—," he asked.

"Yes, it's myrrh!" cried Eliza.

"Do you want *me* to get it?" Darwin asked.

"It's my present," said Eliza. "I'll get it."

Slowly she climbed up. Finally, she reached a sturdy branch, scraped off some sap and tore off some leaves.

"Eliza, now!" cried Marianne. "You didn't need to climb up to get him. Come down, Donnie."

"Well done, Eliza," whispered Darwin.

"Debbie, dear," Marianne called. She pounded on the Commvee door.

"What?" shrieked Debbie, as she flung open the door.

"Please come out, luv," said Nigel.

Debbie walked around the Commvee looking at the decorations. "It's kind of quirky. I like it!" she announced.

Marianne and Nigel gave her their gifts.

"I have a present, too," said Eliza. "It's myrrh to make perfume."

"Hmm. It'll do until we get to civilization," Debbie said. Then she smiled. "What a family."

"What did she say?" Darwin asked Eliza.

Eliza whispered to him as Marianne and Nigel started to sing "Happy Birthday."

"Eliza! *All* she can say is 'It'll do'?" shouted Darwin.

"That's Debbie-language. It means 'I love it,'" Eliza explained.

"Humans are crazy!" Darwin muttered.

"Hey! *What* is that chimp carrying on about?" asked Debbie.

"Oh, he's just trying to sing," said Eliza as she winked at Darwin.